I0614006

Shallow Hill

Jeffery Martin Botzenhart

ALL RIGHTS RESERVED

No part of this book may be reproduced or
transmitted in any form or by any means,
electronic or mechanical, including
photocopying, recording, or by any
information storage and retrieval system,
without permission in writing from the
author, except in the case of brief quotations
embodied in reviews.

Publisher's Note:

This is a work of fiction. All names,
characters, places, and events are the work
of the author's imagination.

Any resemblance to real persons, places, or
events is coincidental.

Solstice Publishing -
www.solsticepublishing.com

Copyright 2017 – Jeffery Martin Botzenhart

Shallow Hill

Jeffery Martin Botzenhart

Chapter One

While treading across the crisp, white snow, all Brianna could hear were brittle crackling sounds. The covering of bare tree branches overhead offered the appearance of death's frail hands disturbed by robust gusts of wind. She lightly traced her fingertips across the cold black iron fence while wandering toward the entrance of the Wyndham Graveyard. Frigid gales had smoothed and shaped the freshly fallen snow to sculptured mounds over the hallowed ground. A few of the larger headstones protruded through the white abyss.

Brianna silently passed through the gates, moving beyond the lower graves to a higher secluded knoll which she referred to as Shallow Hill. This somber point, overlooking the winter-glazed Warwick River, was where she sought out her friends, always bound to this place.

Of all the sites within the Wyndham Graveyard, Shallow Hill was once reserved for those of higher social standings whom had passed on. For a time, it held an aura of opulence with regards to both the quality and artistic expressions of the headstones. Yet with the passing of many years, the affluent luster of Shallow Hill regretfully faded. The original pristine white facades of all the headstones had altered to stained shades of black and ashen grey. Two cherubs, beautifully decorative at one time, had weathered so severely, they now appeared as menacing demons. The statue of a faithful hound deteriorated to the impression of Satan's vile bitch. And a sublime engraved rendering of the Virgin Mary distorted in a resemblance to the Angel of Death. Magnificence once displayed succumbed to be ominously viewed as a profane stone garden.

As Brianna approached her destination, a snowy-white owl took flight from its perch atop the tallest headstone. Unfurling its wings, it majestically glided through the sky until blending into the pale hues of the clouds overhead. She watched it disappear while removing her woolen cloak and then frolicking across the hallowed ground. "Greetings to one and all," Brianna happily called out, the lilt of her voice echoing through the chilled air. Making her way to the first gravestone, she casually brushed the snow off before asking, "Silas and Lott, are you there?"

An argument arose between the two, their spirit voices clearly heard. "Mother said I was the more handsome of us," Silas proudly commented.

"She was always rather daft," Lott responded with noticeable irritation.

"Gentlemen," Brianna interjected, "I am certain you were both quite fetching when you were alive."

Being conjoined twins, only their heads held a slight difference in appearance.

Skipping through the snow, Brianna approached the next headstone. "Good afternoon, Amelia."

"Good afternoon, Brianna," the spirit voice answered through a rather subdued tone. "Do be a dear and check on Captain Bainbridge and Celeste. Something vexes them to no end today."

Strolling over to a larger headstone and brushing the snow from its façade, a polite honorable bow preceded her greeting. "Good afternoon, Captain Bainbridge."

After a moment's hesitation his deep spirit voice emitted a warning. "Do not linger here, my lady. A foul essence taints these grounds. Something evil lurks within the shadows. Something wicked has spoiled the serenity. Beware."

Startled by his warning, Brianna moved on to the farthest headstone. Treading closer, she heard the spirit's faint sobbing. "Celeste, dearest, why do you weep?"

There was anguish expressed within the quivering ghostly voice. "My jewelry is gone. All that remains is a strand of rosaries held by my hands. The thievery occurred during the night when the moon was high. My treasures are no more." The spirit voice returned to its sobbing.

"Who, dearest, would be so cruel to desecrate your resting place?"

"*The marauders*!" Celeste agonizingly wailed out.

Brianna gazed down at the ground nearest to Celeste's headstone. Though partially covered by new fallen snow, there were unmistakable traces of footprints surrounding her resting place. The ground also appeared to have been disturbed. Unladylike words silently stung her tongue as she understood who the thieves were. And she knew just where to find the loathsome fools. A trip to the Black Falcon, a less than reputable tavern frequented by equally less than reputable patrons would be her destination.

As Brianna turned away, Captain Bainbridge issued yet another warning. "They were not alone. His dark shadow was cast near their treachery."

"Who?"

"Ezekiel Fagan."

A chill ran down Brianna's spine when she thought of this man. Unusually tall and thin, shoulder-length hair as white as a phantom, deeply penetrating dark eyes, and an aged smile expressing nothing less than malice was his formidable appearance. Ezekiel Fagan, the village mortician, presented himself as an imposing figure who all appeared to cower under when near him. The responsibility as caretaker for Wyndham Graveyard rested upon his shoulders. In judgment of the graveyard's decrepit condition, one could say his resolve to oversee this task proved to be severely lacking.

Brianna found her woolen cloak and draped it over her shoulders. Briskly, she began walking away through the graveyard with thoughts of her destination clear in her mind, resolving to make certain justice would befall upon the marauders for their thievery. As for Ezekiel Fagan, for the moment she was unsure how to approach him about his treachery.

Reaching a cobblestone path near the river, Brianna's steps were halted when she saw someone sitting on a bench next to the river. Staying hidden among a cluster of trees and bushes, she lingered for some time while watching him. Seldom ever had she spotted anyone sitting near the river during winter. Her suspicions would not have been piqued were it any other season.

"Why are you watching me? Will you not reveal yourself?"

Kindness in the manner by which he grinned captivated her. His adorable dimples exuded a boyish charm while his chiseled jaw contrasted for a more rugged appearance. A cold wind wisped his short auburn hair as if an invisible hand had playfully passed lightly through it. He was quite strikingly handsome.

"Possibly you are a hideous ogre," he added.

"I am no ogre!" Brianna unleashed her indignation over his last remark while bursting through the bushes where she had hidden.

A hearty laugh escaped him as she stood there with her hands firmly planted on her hips. Immediately she began to fret, realizing her foolhardy response had resulted in revealing her presence to him. His beaming smile remained as he sat there on an iron bench, a black quilt covering his legs.

"You are most welcome to sit with me." He patted the empty space next to him. Brianna weakly smiled before slowly wandering over to join him.

Hesitantly, she glanced in his direction. "Never was it my intention to spy on you. I was simply curious as to why you are sitting out here in the cold?" she asked. "For the longest time, you were lost in your thoughts."

"Thoughts are much easier to sift through in quiet places," he responded. "My manners seem to have failed me as I believe an introduction is in order. My name is Pierce." He extended his hand to her.

"Brianna," she said, completing their handshake.

"A very pretty name," he commented, slightly glancing away with endearing shyness.

"I assure you, sir, there is nothing pretty about me." Brianna nervously pushed her full mane of long un-brushed red hair away from her face. Her hand traced down her freckled cheek before coming to rest within her lap. Prior her mother's death two years ago, Brianna had been repeatedly admonished by her for being a larger-sized girl who simply enjoyed a few to many confections.

"I believe the contrary," Pierce remarked, smiling while glancing back at her.

Feeling the need to pull his attention away from her appearance, Brianna asked,

"So… what thoughts have you been lost to? I imagine one or possibly two pretty damsels dream of someone as handsome as you to come to their rescue."

Pierce's smile faded slightly. "I do not believe they would dream of a young man such as me." He removed his quilt, revealing metal braces surrounding his legs, running the length from his thighs to his feet.

"Oh!" She immediately regretted her unthinking comment.

"When I was a boy I stumbled into the path of a charging horse. Both of my legs were broken. I sustained irreversible damage to the muscles surrounding them. Only by the use of these metal braces am I able to walk. After seeing this… most *damsels* tend to run in the opposite direction."

"I believe the contrary," she echoed his remark, causing him a much more pleasant smile.

Brianna visibly struggled to say anything else. Pierce appeared to recognize her distress, returning to the topic of her question. "I am a student at the Essex Academy, in the study of business affairs. I am doing quite poorly with regards to my studies… as I lack any and all passion for them. As for why I was so lost to my thoughts, my father will be arriving by ship this evening for consultations with the chancellor of the academy. Efforts will be discussed in how to improve my disposition about my education."

"Why do you attend the academy if it makes you so unhappy?" Brianna questioned.

"Social obligations, I imagine. Being the son of a brilliant lawyer presents itself with responsibilities to both family and status. Certain choices made for my future… were not choices I would have wished for myself."

"What would you rather be?"

Pierce grinned. "A farmer. I have fond memories of my grandfather's farm in the country. I cherished the times of digging in the dirt by his side and tending to the sheep and fowl. He passed away several years ago. I imagine you would think of me as being mad should I to tell you his spirit came to me one night?"

"Not at all," Brianna quickly replied.

Pierce appeared lost in his thoughts. "One night I was awakened by him calling my name. I sat up in bed and found him sitting next to me. We talked for the longest time over nothing of importance. We simply talked. The next morning I was told by my parents that he had passed away hours before he had visited me." After a quiet moment passed, he broke the silence. "Well… I suppose I should return to the academy and await my fate."

"*Possibly*… you could delay your fate. *Possibly*… you would like to meet my friends?" Brianna asked with hopeful apprehension. "They are not far from here."

"I would very much like that." With slight difficulty he stood up, extending his hand to help her from her seat.

"Thank you," she responded to his chivalry.

His gait was slowed by his leg braces as they walked toward the graveyard. Once they arrived, he cautiously glanced at her. "Your friends are *here*?"

"Yes. They are waiting up at Shallow Hill."

"Shallow Hill?"

"Yes, on the hill at the top of Wyndham Graveyard. I refer to it as the Shallow Hill," Brianna remarked with her usual lilt in her voice.

"You meet your friends… in a graveyard?"

"My friends are always there. Would you like to meet them?"

"Yes. Please lead the way."

Brianna took hold of his hand, assisting him up the snow-covered path. As they drew closer, she could hear the spirit voices of her friends. Amelia commented upon how handsome Brianna's male companion was. Silas and Lott were rather unimpressed as they continued with their earlier argument.

"Your friends appear to have left."

Brianna smiled. "No. They are very much present. They are rather… particular… whom they chose to reveal themselves to." Hesitantly, Brianna admitted, "I have a gift that allows me to converse with the departed. At times I see them, should they wish to be seen. I have other gifts as well. I am what some refer to as a conjurer."

She waited for his reaction. A short escaping laugh preceded his smile.

"You do not believe me. You require proof." She turned away from him, strolling over to Amelia's resting place. After a short whispered conversation Brianna returned to Pierce. "Amelia claims that within your pocket rests your grandfather's gold watch. She also said you have a very nice bare chest."

Cautiously Pierce reached into his pocket and pulled out the gold watch.

"May I see it?" Brianna asked.

"The watch… or the bare chest?"

"Both," she quickly said, an embarrassed glow cast across her face. "The watch, please," she requested as her courage to look at him failed her.

He handed the watch to her. Brianna delicately studied it before returning it to him.

"Do you believe me?" she asked.

"Yes. You believed *me* when I told the story of my grandfather's visit."

"Of course I did."

Appearing curious, he asked, "So… would a conjurer be a sort of witch?"

"I am *no* witch," Brianna replied with slight annoyance. "I am a conjurer. There is a difference. Witches embrace darkness and are servants of Satan."

"I never meant to offend you."

She instantly regretted her reprimand. "I am not offended," she softly replied.

Pierce took a few steps and looked around. "Why do you refer to this place as the Shallow Hill?"

"The ground we stand upon is much harder than down below. The graves here are close to the surface, shallow. Down there, the graves are dug much deeper."

Pierce nodded. "Why do their spirits linger here? Why have they not moved on?"

Brianna thought over this for a moment. "There are several reasons why a spirit lingers amongst the living. The most prominent are they simply cannot give up a life they so long to return to. Another reason would be there is no one waiting to greet them in Heaven."

"Why would their spirits be bound to this place? What hinders their freedom to travel other places?"

"The spirits *here* are bound by personal treasures they were buried with. For example, Captain Bainbridge was laid to rest with his sword, a possession he greatly coveted when alive. Spirits unable to ascend to Heaven *can* in fact travel from one place to another if there remains another possession of great value to them somewhere near or far. Certain spirits watch over a family member who may have inherited these coveted possessions… while others haunt the living they view as undeservingly to have received or purchased cherished items, anything from jewelry to furniture."

A smile beamed from Pierce's face as he looked to her. "Be you a conjurer or a witch, I believe you have cast an enchantment over me."

"How so?" she asked in concern.

"I would very much like to kiss you," he boldly answered. A heavy snow began to descend upon them. "Well... I should be going. Thank you for leading me here."

Walking over to him, Brianna placed a soft kiss upon his cheek, noticing the blush flitting across his handsome face.

"To further complicate your thoughts," she playfully said with a smile.

Pierce slowly walked away, turning back once to wave to her. Moments later, he disappeared as the flurry of snow became a squall.

Chapter Two

A solemn expression adorned Ezekiel Fagan's wrinkled face while addressing a distraught gentleman. Every word sounded meticulously spoken, the nuances of each syllable uttered with perfection. His speech held a slowly practiced, calculated tone.

"You have my deepest sympathy over your dreadful untimely loss. The death of someone... so very young and fragile is... unfathomable."

The gentleman sitting across from him glanced away, his unspoken words appearing blocked within his throat. After a struggle of several silent moments one word found release. "How?"

Ezekiel Fagan entwined his bone-thin fingers as his expression altered to thoughtfulness. "Two men under my employment witnessed the unfortunate incident. It appeared your son grew disoriented within a snow squall as he was walking along the Warwick River. Somehow... he wandered off the path... and found himself standing upon the frozen river. The solid surface then cracked. Your son plunged below the ice... into the freezing depths. By the time my men made it out to the hole in the ice... he had drowned. Had he not been wearing his metal leg braces... then perhaps... he could have treaded the icy water longer."

More moments of silence followed. Ezekiel Fagan released a deep sigh before continuing. "I will need your son's full name for the certificate of death."

Through trembling words the man uttered, "Pierce... Alden... Fleming."

After writing this down, Ezekiel Fagan commenced with more details needing to be satisfied. "I greatly regret I must trouble you in your hour of despair over arrangements for both the funeral and the burial."

"I will be returning home with his body for a proper burial near our family estate."

Once more, Ezekiel Fagan entwined his bone-thin fingers as he thoughtfully looked at the man. "I greatly understand your desire to have your son's final resting place close by. However... what you suggest may lead to certain... complications. In the past, I have been informed that many a mariner would object to such a cargo... as it invokes ill fortune upon the ship. Not to mention the further stress you will suffer through," he added. "I urge you to reconsider. The Wyndham Graveyard truly holds breathtaking serenity for one's final resting place."

Breaking down with uncontrolled sobbing, the man finally abandoned his plans for returning home with his son's body. All the necessary paperwork was signed with payment being made in full for Ezekiel Fagan's services.

"My son had a gold pocket watch given to him by his grandfather. I would see its return to me," the man requested.

"I am… terribly sorry. We found no such watch with your son. If he did not leave it with his belongings at the Essex Academy… then most likely is at rest within the depths of the Warwick River."

The man's expression appeared to worsen upon hearing this.

"May I see my son's face before I leave?"

"I would not suggest this," Ezekiel Fagan responded. "Please understand his body was severely frozen. I would… much rather you remember how he looked in youthful health rather than your final memory of him… being in death."

The man nodded his head in understanding before his hasty departure. Ezekiel Fagan watched from the window until the man's carriage disappeared from sight. Turning away from outside, he placed his hand into his pocket and playfully caressed the gold coins.

Loud frantic knocking upon another door leading into his study disturbed Ezekiel Fagan from this quiet moment. After opening the door a well-dressed man entered, proceeding to pace the length of the room.

"Chancellor Billingsly, how fortunate for you to visit this evening. Please, I simply… implore you to follow me."

Ezekiel Fagan, with the chancellor pursuing closely, left the study. Before reaching the back door, they came to a halt at the center of a long hallway. Ezekiel Fagan knelt down, moving a carpet out of the way in revealing a trap door. Pulling the floorboards up, a dark staircase was revealed underneath. Ezekiel Fagan took hold of a kerosene lamp from a side table. Together, the men descended the stairs to a dark and damp chamber below.

A metal door shone opened as they stepped into a much darker room with no windows. The mist of their warm breath escaped before their eyes within the frigid air. Ezekiel Fagan led the chancellor to the farthest wall of the room. The chancellor's eyes grew large when viewing what was waiting there for him.

"Have I satisfied an insatiable craving… within you? Is this not worth yet another fortune?"

The chancellor spoke no words, acting as if his throat proved barren of moisture.

"Oh, how dreadful. He is not to your liking." Ezekiel Fagan ran his hand across the young man's bare chest and stomach before tracing it up to his face and through his damp hair. The young man made no movement with exception of his shallow breathing, noticeable from the rise and fall of his chest. The gentle cascade of freezing water near him offered the room's only other sound.

"Possibly… your preference is for a fair-haired young man… as you purchased the last time? Such a pity it was… that he survived the hunt… yet did not survive your carnal infatuation. Yet I am certain you extracted pleasure with every… exquisite… ounce of his agony."

Hesitantly, the chancellor reached out his hand to touch the young man's bare flesh. Ezekiel Fagan abruptly halted this.

"As chancellor, you are indeed aware that not all rules… are meant to be broken.

One must not touch… what one has not purchased. Is our price agreed upon?"

Without speaking, the chancellor nodded his head in approval. A silent handshake sealed their fate with this dark endeavor.

†††

"What are we doing in a church?" Egan Craven asked through slurred drunken words.

Peter Borgan, his partner in crime, splashed holy water on his face before indulging in more spirits. Brianna twirled and danced up the aisle of the sanctuary, stopping and turning back once she had reached the altar.

"Well, my lover, if I am to make the ultimate sacrifice of my virtue, what better place than a church?" she replied to Egan.

"I will drink to that," Egan said and did.

Brianna had traveled to the Black Falcon in search of these two marauders. Yet before seeking them out, she returned to her cottage outside of the city for a potion-laced bottle of spirits for the two. The tongues of drunken men spilled many a secret. Adding a truth serum would offer clarity as well as the resolve to comply with her every demand without question.

"Do you not desire me?" she breathlessly asked, exposing her breasts to the men.

"A bit on the heavy side you are," Peter commented before finishing the spirits in his bottle and casting it aside."

"More of me for your pleasure," she replied, suppressing her anger.

Egan walked up to her, attempting to cop a feel, yet she would have none of it. From a basket she carried with her, Brianna pulled out the bottle of spirits she had brought for the men. After popping the cork, she tempted Egan with the bottle.

"This is no ordinary spirit, my lover. This was made with the nectar of forbidden fruits. Why the devil, himself, would happily recite holy scripture... with just a taste upon his lips," Brianna breathlessly enticed.

She had told the truth, as the requirement of the elixir dictated for full potency. A drunkenly-wicked smile cast across Egan's face when taking the bottle from her.

"Drink up, my lovers. The night is young," she seductively purred.

Egan took a large gulp from the bottle, before handing it to Peter. Within minutes, the marauders consumed every drop of the spirits. The time had now arrived to test its potency.

"Remove your clothes," Brianna firmly commanded.

Through noticeable bewilderment, the men complied with her demand and were soon standing naked before her.

"Oh my." In reference to their endowments, she mumbled, "Some tall tales are in fact rather short stories."

With their eyes fully glazed, Brianna surmised the men had fallen under the full influence of the potion. Thus began her interrogation of them with the lilt of her voice holding a more serious tone. "You will speak only the truth when answering my questions. Now then, were you two the thieves who stole jewelry from the grave of Celeste Coleville?"

"Yes," they responded in unison.

"And... did you have an accomplice in this endeavor?"

Again in unison they responded, "Yes."

"Was your accomplice Ezekiel Fagan?"

Both answered, "Yes."

Peter appeared to fall asleep while standing there. This was a side effect of the potion when consumed with large quantities of ale and rum. Understanding Egan would soon fall asleep as well, Brianna asked him one final question. "Where is Celeste's jewelry?"

"Hidden within Ezekiel Fagan's study," Egan whispered before falling to a deep sleep while standing there just as Peter was.

Having her questions answered with satisfaction, Brianna next extracted her revenge upon the marauders. Silently she led Peter to the altar where she helped him lay before the many rows of pews. Once content with his position she then lured Egan over to Peter, positioning his naked body in a manner most improper for a church setting.

"My lovers, I do not envy you the embarrassment and punishment you will so deservedly receive when Father Beatty discovers your carnal embrace at sunrise." She blew them a kiss before quietly departing.

Chapter Three

The cloud cover had dissipated enough for the moon to appear overhead within the dark night sky. While passing through the graveyard, Brianna observed how the strong north wind disturbed the fallen snow on Shallow Hill. A wintery vortex ascended into the crisp air before fading away as if a phantom vanishing before her eyes.

Within an hour of leaving the marauders in the church, Brianna found her way to the funeral parlor where Ezekiel Fagan conducted business. Granite statues of two sitting lions anchored a grand stone staircase leading to the large front doors. The weathered-grey stone façade of the building and darkened windows displayed a most inhospitable aura. Walking past the front of the building, she then headed down a darkened side alley. From a pocket on her dress, Brianna pulled out a skeleton key. By chance, she had found it in the graveyard during the warm season. Driven by mischief and curiosity over time, Brianna discovered each and every door throughout the city could be opened with it. She never wondered why the skeleton key, in fact, existed. Many things existed in this world that lacked explanation. Yet, she was thankful on this night to have it in her possession.

Holding her breath, Brianna placed the key into a lock on the back door of the funeral parlor. After a deep exhale, she turned the key and the lock silently opened for her. With extreme caution, she pushed the door in before lightly stepping inside, closing it behind her.

Overwhelming fragrances of candles and formaldehyde assaulted her nostrils, causing her to shield her nose with her cloak for a moment. Stepping over to a table flooded with moonlight penetrating through a nearby window, she picked up a candle and ran her hand above the wick. After whispering a faint incantation, a flame immediately ignited, bathing the room with its soft flickering glow. She had entered a storage room with several caskets in various stages of finish. Though some might have found discomfort in such surroundings, Brianna felt completely at ease. Yet there was no time to linger.

Into a darkened hallway Brianna stepped as she searched for Ezekiel Fagan's study. After opening two doors, she found what she sought behind a third. Warmth not shared with the rest of the funeral parlor flooded over her from a fire, much too intensely burning within the fireplace. Exhaling her held breath once inside, she frantically rummaged through his desk drawers. No care was given for disturbing the numerous letters and a death certificate littering his desktop.

Resounding footsteps drawing closer pulled Brianna away from her search. Dousing the flame of her candle, she found refuge behind a large brown curtain. She remained still as she heard the footsteps enter into the study. Peering out slightly, Brianna spied Ezekiel Fagan withdrawing a large wooden box from atop a tall bookshelf. Using a key he pulled out from his pocket, he opened the lid and carelessly dropped something inside. He then used the key to lock the box before returning it to its place atop the bookshelf. Ezekiel Fagan appeared fatigued as he rubbed his temple. A moment later he left, closing the door behind him.

Quickly relighting the candle, Brianna cautiously carried a chair over to the bookshelf, climbing upon the seat. Her fingertips just barely reached the top shelf. With great care, she inched the box to the edge, allowing for a better grasp to lower it. Quietly, she set it down on the desk. After a brief examination, Brianna pulled the skeleton key from her pocket, placing in in the lock. As she suspected, the key turned with ease. Opening the heavy lid, Brianna gazed with a mixture of both wonder and despair over the contents. Gold coins, precious gems, and ornate jewelry filled the box to its brim. One particular piece caught her eye.

"It cannot be his," she whispered with slight concern.

A gold pocket watch, identical to the one Pierce carried, rested next to a diamond pendant. She dismissed any thought of it belonging to him. Another piece of jewelry, one she instantly recognized without doubt, was also within her sight. Her heart sank further as she picked it up; studying the ornately decorated locket her mother had worn. Forcing it into a pocket of her dress, she understood the need to clear her mind and continue on with her task. A time would come later when she could revisit the mournful loss of her mother and father, still brutally painful.

Dragging her thoughts back, what proved uncertain to her was exactly which jewelry belonged to Celeste. Clearly certain, she knew that none of these treasures belonged to Ezekiel Fagan. Brianna also believed Celeste's resting place may not have been the only grave to have been plundered. After a thoughtful moment,

Brianna came to the decision to steal away with the box and its contents. Although uncertain as to how she would see to the return any of these belongings to their rightful owners, she resolved to try with the help of her spirit friends.

Stepping out into to the dark hallway, Brianna halted when she spied the presence of a young blonde-haired man standing before the large front doors. Barefoot and shirtless, she saw countless bruises and lacerations marring his bare back. His injuries appeared excruciatingly painful yet he seems oblivious to them. The mannerisms expressed by his body language offered the dual impressions of curiosity and apprehension. As Brianna took a step toward him, the floorboards emitted sounds alerting him that he was not alone. Slowly turning toward her, the glow from her candle revealed injuries to his face and chest, similar to those upon his back.

"Who did this to you?" Brianna's voice quivered with sorrow for him.

"I never saw his face. He wore a mask," the young man faintly whispered.

Immediately Brianna recognized the quality of his tone. It was similar to that of the spirits from Shallow Hill. The young man was in fact a spirit bound to this place.

"What is your name?"

"Byron Tannehill."

"Why are you here?"

"I do not know how to —leave—or where to go if I could," he quietly responded.

"You precious angel, I could show you the way," Brianna offered, kindly smiling at him through her unyielding tears.

"What of the other? He is not yet dead."

The moisture in her throat evaporated as her body forcefully quaked with a chill. "There is another... here?"

"In the oubliette," Byron whispered. "Find the trap door and descend into the darkness below. There is where you will find him."

Brianna walked up to Byron, standing at his side. Through her own whispered words she hesitantly asked, "Who will I find?"

The young man did not answer her question, appearing distracted by a sound. "Do you hear that?"

Brianna, in fact, did hear something, the barking of a dog echoing from close by.

"I believe the sound is coming from outside," she responded.

"No, it sounds as if from a dream," Byron corrected her. His eyes grew large as a smile adorned his face. "I see blue skies with white clouds and an open field of goldenrod. I see my dog from when I was a child. I —believe—that it wants me to come to it. May I?"

Tears continued flowing from Brianna's eyes as she whispered, "You simply must."

"Is it like this for everyone?"

"No, angel, this is only for you." Brianna leaned over, placing a soft kiss on his cheek. This left a tingling sensation upon her lips. "Welcome home, Byron. Go on with you."

His spirit form began to disappear, yet not before he turned back to her. "Find him. Do not allow his fate to be that of mine. Promise me."

"*I—promise*," Brianna's voice quaveringly responded.

Turning away, her breath rushed from her as she stumbled backwards, startled by the apparitions of departed men, women, and children lining the hallway. The somber expressions of each gripped her with an overwhelming sense of dread.

"So many souls linger here in this terrible place," she said.

The ghostly form of an elderly man glided forward. "There is no time for despair, my lady. Not—when one can still be saved."

Placing her fingers to her lips, Brianna asked, "And what of all of you. How can I find release for your souls?"

A young woman with long flowing hair moved forward, replying with the saddest of smiles. "We are beyond your reach—until the light of Heaven arrives for each of us—someday."

"Save the boy—from a most dreadful fate," the elderly man urged.

"Will you lead me to where he is?"

"No, my lady; were our souls to cross the threshold into that damned chamber, we would suffer interment into Hell for eternity. Make haste! His breathing grows shallow," the elderly man responded.

Brianna watched as each spirit form then vanished from sight. Never had she felt more alone than at this moment.

Chapter Four

A loud thump from upstairs startled Brianna. Tripping over her feet, stumbling face first upon the floor, the wooden box she held was sent flying into the air. Fortunately it landed with only a light thud. However, the lid was jarred open, sending the contents sprawling across the carpets.

Brianna remained still, awaiting any reaction from upstairs for the noise she'd made. After agonizing moments passed with silence, she gathered the spilled jewelry and coins. Light from a streetlamp that shone in from a window next to the front door aided her in collecting what had spilled from within the box.

When she stood up, her foot kicked something, launching it down the dark hallway. Using her feet, this time, she cautiously tapped the floor in search of the lost object. Moving to the hallway's center, her shoe tapped what she was in search of and more. The faint echo of her tapping noticeably changed as if the floor was somehow different at this point, though the carpet that ran the length of the hall hid this.

Bending down, she picked up the object, rediscovering the gold pocket watch.

A chill caressed her fingers as they touched the carpet. Tapping her fist lightly against the floor boards, she noticed the unmistakable hollowness in the sound it made. Suddenly, Byron's words resonated in her ears. She had found the trap door he spoke of.

Kneeing down, Brianna pulled the carpet aside and searched with her fingers for a latch. A rush of cold damp air made her body shudder as the hatch opened. The subtle glow from a light down below illuminated a narrow stone spiral staircase. Inhaling a deep breath for courage, she eased her foot down onto the first step. Once far enough inside, she pulled the trap door closed.

The dampness coating the mostly darkened steps proved hazardous to descend. Twice her foot slipped out from under her. Had it not been for her tight grip on the railing, she would have plummeted to the unseen bottom.

Brianna allowed her breathing to relax once she reached the stone floor below. There sitting upon a small wooden table was a candle with but only a few more moments of wax left. A windowless metal door separated the staircase from an adjoining room; the surface was glazed with cold water drops. She touched the door handle, finding it locked. Once more she relied upon the use of her skeleton key.

Slowly she turned the key. Brianna pushed the door open as the hinges wailed out excruciating screeching sounds. Her heart nearly exploded through her chest when she warily stepped into the room. Splashing upon her face were tiny droplets of moisture. The sound of cascading water resounded from the darkest corner of the room. Treading one small step after the next, she lowered the candle down toward the floor. As she reached the farthest corner, light from the candle revealed bare feet. The trembling of her hand caused the flame to frantically flicker when she summoned her courage to raise the light. A dark, damp pair of men's trousers was revealed to her. Tears streamed down her cheeks as the light shone upon a young man's bare muscular stomach and chest. Lastly, Brianna stifled her sorrowful scream when the light showed upon Pierce's face.

Her vision blurred. She uncontrollably wept before him. His arms were held high over his head; his hands were bound in shackles to iron chains. The frigid cascading water relentlessly soaked his body from head to toe. Severe bruises and a blackened eye marred his once handsome face. Fearfully, she reached out, placing her hand softly upon his skin. Immediately she recoiled, feeling the faint beating of his heart and the shallow rise and fall of his chest.

Unable to control her relief, Brianna vigorously embraced him as her tears of sorrow turned to joy. The sensation of his warm breath fell upon her neck. So overcome with emotions, she placed a passionate kiss upon his cold lips. Slipping from her grasp, the candle dropped to a puddle of water below Pierce's dangling feet, though not extinguishing.

"I must save you," she desperately whispered.

Through the darkness she reached up, her fingertips revealing a padlock that bound the chains to his hands. Thinking fast, once more she pulled out the skeleton key from her pocket. However, a scream of agony burst from her when she discovered it would not fit into the lock. Exhaling with defeat, Brianna took a step back, running her hands through her long red hair. As her hand reached the crown of her head, her fingers encountered something dangling from above. Reached up, her palm caressed a much smaller key. Her mind instantly understood the devilry with this. The key to his escape had torturously been placed there before him, only inches away from his grasp.

"Eternal damnation upon your soul, Ezekiel Fagan," Brianna rasped, retrieving the smaller key and forcing it into the lock.

Pierce's body fell quickly upon her, yet her robust strength caught and cradled him within her arms. She understood the need to hold strength for both of them as his metal leg braces were missing and his unconscious state rendered him unable to move on his own. Though the task was slow and difficult, Brianna struggled in managing to pull him from the darkened room and up the damp staircase.

She rested his body down upon the hallway floor, then closed the trap door and replaced the carpet over it. She waited in silence for sounds from upstairs. All was quiet. Pulling Pierce up and heaving his arm across her shoulders, she gradually returned to the back door. Before departing, Brianna wrapped his body with her wool cloak in an effort to keep him as warm as possible.

The city's hospital, on High Street near the port, was several blocks away. Brianna quickly dismissed any thoughts of taking Pierce there. She knew well how Ezekiel Fagan stalked the infirmary and convalescent wings, offering his services as needed when patients died. A horrific notion crossed her mind, wondering if those who passed away did so by natural causes—or if somehow Ezekiel Fagan *assisted* in a most untimely fashion with their deaths.

Another thought, one to report this crime to the constable, was also quickly rejected. Constable Ratcliff had an unusual rapport with Ezekiel Fagan, at times both appearing as thick as thieves with their hushed conversations. Many saw him as a man above reproach, yet she found him guilty by association. Having always known the citizens of Charlesburg viewed her wearily due to her odd upbringing as the daughter of a magician and a fortuneteller, Brianna understood she would find neither welcome nor assistance from anyone in the city. Only by taking Pierce away with her to her home in the forest could she offer him safety.

Farther down the alley she spotted a coal wagon, leading Pierce to it and then helping him on. Brianna's pace in getting as far away as possible was hindered by a sudden deluge of snow upon the city. Yet the adrenaline coursing through her fueled her strength as they silently passed house by house before escaping into the snowy night.

Several times as they trekked deeper into the forest, she stopped to check on Pierce. The quaking of his body appeared to intensify as his diminished breathing grew more distressed. The paleness of his skin also greatly alarmed her. Yet a faint murmur from his lips allowed her heart to beat faster. She kissed his head before returning to her task. Brianna's pace quicken through the unrelenting snowfall. A terrible chill coursed through her own body as the wintry deluge stung her exposed flesh.

Pressing onward with difficulty through the ever deepening drifts, her sense of hope began to wane.

"Will there be no end to this?" she asked as a tear fell from her eye to freeze upon her cheek.

The forest had always been her refuge, yet on this night it betrayed her. For a time, she failed to recognize any reminders of her way home until crossing paths with a stream where she cooled herself in the warm seasons, now shrouded by winter's blanket. A brisk north wind assaulted the treetops, forcing their limbs and branches to perform a chaotic ballet. Her celestial guides were blocked from view by barely visible clouds. Only the faint outline of the winter moon daringly shone through the squalls, yet for how long?

As time slowly passed, she continued, treading deeper and deeper into the forest. Stumbling over a rock hidden under the snow, Brianna fell to her knees. Upon standing up, she joyfully caught sight of her chimney in the not too far distance. With her hope restored, she uttered through chattering teeth, "We—ar-re—almost—ther-re."

A deep snowbank halted the coal wagon only a short way from her cottage. Heaving him up, Brianna dragged Pierce until she reached the door. With what strength remained in her, she forced the door open. They both collapsed upon her floor. She forcefully kicked it closed behind her.

The warmth of a low fire intensified as Brianna placed two logs upon the flames. Quickly turning her attention back to Pierce, she helped him to her bed. Removing his remaining clothes, she tucked him underneath a thick quilt in effort to warm his frozen body. Throughout the following hour, she added several more quilts and placed hot coals in a bedpan, carefully positioning it under her mattress. She understood how his body would require a gradual warming so as to not stop his heart by the immediate embrace of heat.

Over to the fireplace she went, resting near the roaring flames. From inside the wooden box, she found Pierce's gold pocket watch. Holding it within her outstretched hands toward the fire, she lightly spoke in another tongue, an ancient dialect. Invoking an enchantment, the pocket watch was transformed into a talisman she attached to a golden chain. Brianna rose, rushing to Pierce's side. Carefully she placed the talisman over his head so it would hang from around his neck.

His coloration had slightly improved yet the quaking of his body had not lessened. After covering him with one more quilt, she made a rather bold decision. Another source of heat she would use was body heat. Brianna stripped off her own clothes, crawling naked under the quilts next to him. Pulling Pierce close, she offered the warmth her body held for him. And as time passed, with her strength depleted, she fell into a deep sleep wrapped within his arms.

Chapter Five

How long he had been asleep, Pierce was uncertain. He felt terrible aching pains from his head to his feet; the throbbing of his arms was the most severe. Believing hours had passed, his mind yielded no memories but one exception. He remembered Brianna. He had not felt such exhilaration in many a year after meeting her in the park next to the Warwick River. He recalled how pretty she was and how she did not feel that way about herself. A flash of memory when he stood in the graveyard with her quickly faded. Pierce tried thinking further about this, but it would not return.

A subtle movement from his side drew his attention. The flames from the fireplace offered just enough light for him to see. Under the quilts next to him, was Brianna's beautiful face. Her full mane of red hair partially covered her cheek. Delicately through considerable pain, Pierce winced, reaching over to gently pull her hair back. Angelic was how best he could describe her sleeping expression. He wished he could remember how they came to be together here yet there was no memory to recall. With growing exhaustion, he snuggled his body next to her, closing his eyes. He hoped this was no dream or possibly one he would not soon awaken from.

Several hours later, as the morning sunlight shone through the cottage windows, Pierce stirred from a restful sleep. He felt the return of some of his strength yet only few of his aches had subsided. Turning his head to the right he saw Brianna was still asleep beside him. Something he also noticed was his arousal for her. He carefully shifted his body so she would not notice.

"Brianna," he whispered, attempting to awaken her.

She made no movement. Leaning his head over, Pierce placed a soft kiss upon her nose. This time her head moved slightly as she mumbled something he could not understand. Smiling at her, he sensed she was amidst a very content dream. He hoped he might be part of it. Leaning over further, he boldly placed a passionate kiss on her full lips, his cheek brushing against hers as his warm exhale cascaded down her neck.

After a moment, her eyes fluttered before finally opening.

"Good morning," Pierce whispered.

Brianna smiled, snuggling closer to him. His attempt to hide his arousal failed when her bare leg draped across his naked body. Her eyes grew wide in apparent shock as she cautiously pulled her leg back. Brianna tugged a quilt close to her as she sat up.

"I should explain," she embarrassingly said without looking at him. Frustratingly covering her face with her hands, she confessed, "I am not certain where to begin."

"You could begin by telling me why you are not looking at me," he responded.

Deeply exhaling, Brianna replied, "If I was to look at —you—then I would be tempted to kiss you."

The awkwardness of her body language caused him to grin.

"I very much wish you would look at me."

††††

Her hesitant glance met the warmth of his smile. Leaning over, his lips faintly brushed across hers as if waiting for her to react. His nose sensually moved from one side of hers to the next, deeply inhaling. Looking into his eyes, she saw his desire for her.

"I know you see your reflection in my eyes. How would you describe it?" Pierce breathlessly whispered.

"How should I describe it?"

"As someone sublimely beautiful," he replied.

"No, that would not be me," she disagreed.

"Why do you hold such shame for how you appear?"

"Beauty and I will never be companions," she responded.

"You are blind."

Awkwardly glancing down, Brianna asked, "How is it you view me in a light others have failed to see?"

Grinning, he answered, "Although I find myself spellbound by your stunning face and pleasurable body, your most lovely feature is your heart. It radiates a glow rivaling that of the sun, yet offering far more warmth. It is *that* which enchants me, casting a spell upon my soul. Your heart is a beacon amidst a dark world, drawing me to you, leaving me craving to taste your lips. If you would allow me to be so bold to ask, may I kiss you again?"

Though embarrassed by such words, her unrestrained yearning to be kissed caused her to utter, "Please."

Delicately at first, their kiss grew to fiery intensity as her hands cradled his chin before roaming down to his chest. He released the quilt covering her. Pulling her lips from his, Brianna could not hide her expression of shame from him. Lifting her chin up so her eyes could meet his, he tenderly whispered, "You are the most beautiful woman I have ever seen. I am hopelessly captivated by you."

Returning with vigor to kissing him, what seemed a sharp pain robbed him of his breath, forcing his body back down to the bed.

"*I have hurt you*," Brianna fretted.

Pierce winced, forcing a smile upon his face.

"No," he replied as he reached his hand up to caress her chin. "I have no memory of why I am in such —pain—or how I came to be here with you."

After saying this, he reached down, finding his pocket watch hanging around his neck. "How did this get here?"

"Please do not take that off." Brianna panicked, her hand coming to rest upon his. "You must understand why some of your memories are hidden from you. You suffered through a terrible ordeal before I found you. I am uncertain as to the how or why of it all. —yet—I fear it would cause great distress for you to relive those moments. To shield you from —this—I cast a memory enchantment upon your pocket watch. While this talisman is worn by you, all sorrowful and terrible memories will be hidden from your thoughts. Should you take it off—these memories will return to you in a most nightmarish manner. I beg you not to take it off," she pleaded.

"I will not remove it. I promise," Pierce whispered, his sincerity most evident.

"I need to test its potency," Brianna added before kissing him once more.

"What do you remember?"

"Our kiss," he happily replied.

She harshly slapped his cheek. "What do you remember?"

"Our kiss," he happily repeated, offering no reaction to her slap.

Satisfied with his answer, Brianna rose from the bed and pulled on her dress. She walked over to a black iron stove and ignited a fire within it before placing a black iron pot on its top.

"You have a cauldron," Pierce commented. "I imagine most witches have one for brewing potions."

Slightly annoyed by this, Brianna responded, "This is a pot. I use this to wash my clothes. As I said before, I am a conjurer—not a witch. There is a difference."

A devilishly playful smile adorned Pierce's face. "Do you have a black cat?"

With growing irritation, she responded, "No. Wretched beasts, cats are. They cause me insufferable sneezing."

"Do you have any warts?"

"Do you see any?" she asked indignantly.

"What about a broom?"

Thoroughly exasperated, Brianna quickly answered, "Yes I *do* and I shall *beat you* with it should you continue to mock me."

His smile and laughter were infectious. She could not help herself from smiling also.

"Promise?" he faintly murmured.

Brianna huffed, attempting to ignore his mischief.

"Do you have a family? he asked, his expression now exuding drowsiness.

"My parents are gone," Brianna responded and turned away from him. "My father was a magician and my mother was a fortuneteller. They traveled extensively with a troupe of other performers from one end of the country to the other. Two years ago, they left for a seaside festival in the far north. They never returned—for reasons I am not certain of."

Knowing she had found her mother's locket with other treasures stolen by the marauders, she now believed that her parents were dead. Not wishing to further burden either her or Pierce with this, Brianna spoke no more of them, banishing these thoughts so as to concentrate on her task.

From a shelf near the window, she pulled down a small bowl and lit the contents within it. A moment later, she returned to Pierce's side, setting the bowl on a table next to the bed. A pleasantly fragrant veil of smoke flowed across the bed.

"What, may I ask, it that?" Pierce asked.

"It is chamomile leaves. The aroma will relax you. You should rest," Brianna said, gently touching his cheek.

"Will you lay with me for a while?"

Without speaking, Brianna snuggled next to him upon the bed. As time passed, Pierce fell into a deep sleep. Later, she pulled herself from his embrace and fetched her cloak. She knew the aroma of the chamomile would keep Pierce asleep for several hours. Fear of leaving his side was regretfully dismissed with other pressing matters forcing her to seek out the lingering spirits of Shallow Hill.

Chapter Six

Ezekiel Fagan quietly stood back as the priest bestowed final rites upon the grave of Pierce Alden Fleming. The young man's father vainly attempted to control his sorrow, standing there alone on the other side of the casket. None of Pierce's classmates, professors, or even Bernard Billingsly, the academy chancellor, had arrived for the mid-morning burial. Cowering several gravesites away were Egan Craven and Peter Borgan, both of whom had been released from their incarceration for trespassing and public indecency charges with Ezekiel Fagan's discreet bribery among prominent church and city officials. Both were notorious for their usual public intoxication. Yet never before had their behavior ended in such a humiliating manner.

Other vexing thoughts distracted Ezekiel Fagan's mind, the most important being that of Pierce's disappearance from the chamber beneath the funeral parlor. He withheld mention of this to the academy chancellor, determined not to risk the loss of a small fortune. There was also the inexplicable theft of his wooden box. No amount of bribery would shield him from charges of theft or public outcry should his gruesome endeavors come to light. Although the circle of those seeking his profane services held important standings in society, he understood how precarious his own position rested. Many were justifiably fearful of him. He relished having such power, yet just as many would welcome retribution for his tyranny.

With his gaze wandering away from sight the empty casket, Ezekiel Fagan caught a glimpse of a young woman strolling among the headstones upon the hill. His suspicions turned rampant when he noticed how she remained nearest to the grave of Celeste Coleville. More intriguing to him, though, was how she appeared to be carrying on a conversation, her head nodding and hands moving with fluidity. His memories returned to that recent night, overseeing the marauders here within the Wyndham Graveyard in the harvesting of valuables from the deceased. Was it possible they were watched when Celeste's grave was robbed of her jewels? His certainty they were alone that night faded. He wondered if he had succumbed to carelessness while blinded by greed.

Turning away from the young woman, Ezekiel Fagan grew alarmed in noticing something else. From his view where he stood, he recognized the proximity of the graveyard to the Warwick River. It was close by where his employees had abducted the young men. With growing unease, Ezekiel Fagan returned his attention to the young woman upon the hill. Be it a fortunate coincidence, he found her staring suspiciously back at him.

"Thank you, Mister Fagan," Pierce's father said, abruptly pulling his attention away from the young woman.

"You have my... deepest sympathy," Ezekiel Fagan said. "I should see you to the port where your ship awaits."

"I would very much like to remain here for a short while," Pierce's father replied.

"As you wish. My employees and I will leave you... and return within the hour." Ezekiel Fagan motioned for the men to follow him away from the casket. Upon reaching the gates, he instructed the men, "Return to the funeral parlor and wait for my arrival."

Once they had left he cautiously made his way back near Pierce's father, yet remaining hidden. His suspicions were further piqued when the young woman slowly approached the fresh grave, allowing him to listen to her conversation.

"A heartbreaking loss you have suffered," she softly commented to Pierce's father.

Attempting to compose himself, he asked, "Were you acquainted with my son?"

"We are friends, I —mean—we *were* friends," she answered.

"When did you last see him?"

"Yesterday afternoon, before the snowstorm."

"I am Malcolm Fleming," Pierce's father said. Did... he... speak of me?"

"Yes. He said you would be visiting. He was very much looking forward to your arrival."

"I sincerely doubt that. He was greatly unhappy in his last correspondence to me. I should offer no —deception—as it would be a sin here before his grave. Pierce was miserable for far too many years. A week at sea allows for clarity of thought. So *blinded* by my ambitions for myself and for —him—I failed to understand what he desired for himself. A part of me wanted to return home with him, find some resolution to our differences, a thoughtful gesture much too late now."

The young woman reached out her hand, thoughtfully taking hold of Pierce's father's. They spoke no more as she offered a kind smile before departing. A moment later Pierce's father bent down to place a kiss upon the casket before turning away and leaving. Ezekiel Fagan cared not for this, as his gaze followed the young woman's path away from the graveyard. He wickedly resolved that her destination would soon become his.

A soothingly warm bath was drawn by Brianna for Pierce. With some difficulty she managed to help him to the tub, easing him into the steamy water. The enchantment placed upon the pocket watch hanging from his neck made it resistant to damage by water, heat, and cold. Sitting next to the tub, she ran a cloth over the aching muscles of his back, neck, and arms. Reaching his arm over, Pierce gently pulled her head over to his so his lips could reach hers. After a passionate kiss was shared he whispered, "Join me, please."

"Promise not to look while I undress," Brianna requested.

"I will make no such promise," he challenged.

Feeling both vexed and exhilarated by his devilishly inviting grin, Brianna hesitantly stood up, unable to deny wanting to be with him. Terrified of being so exposed, all at the same time, Brianna slowly shed her dress to stand naked before him. Her fears of how unattractive she felt were cast away by his smile when he reached for her. Easing her body into the warm water before him, he embraced her as she came to rest against his muscular chest. Cupping her chin gently, he turned her face from side-to-side. He faintly traced his lips across her forehead before descending down her nose to brush against her lips. Boldly she pulled his head forward, sharing one devouring kiss after another. All restraint was lost as she allowed herself the pleasure of feeling beautiful and desirable.

He pulled her close to his body with both releasing pleasurable exhales. The steam from the bath made their skin fell like silk, glistening from the flickering firelight. Brianna ran her hands through his wet hair as their kissing continued. Her yearning to touch him met with no resistance. Pierce controlled her body, enticing rapture from her. The caress of his hands upon her wet flesh proved an ecstasy unlike she had ever known, consuming her. Her heart's rampant beating and labored breathing pushed her to the brink of delirium as their delight intensified. Pierce buried his face against her shoulder, placing soft kisses to her flesh. Brianna's sighs of ecstasy were soon matched with Pierce's, rendering them to a breathless romantic embrace. Attempting to pull free from him, she failed to find release from his arms. His intoxicating grin held her spellbound.

Easing her body away, Pierce's fingers faintly traced over her skin as they soaked in the now cooling water, refreshing to their heated bodies. For a time, no words were exchanged between them, yet troubling thoughts within Brianna's mind cast a pall upon this blissful moment.

Knowing she could no longer withhold these thoughts, Brianna turned her head so she could gaze upon his handsome face. "Do you remember when we met?"

"Of course," he replied. "I was sitting on a bench next to the river. You were hidden behind some bushes, watching me."

"Why were you sitting on that bench?" she softly asked.

Confusion clouded his expression. "I cannot remember why I was there." A smile returned to his face as he looked at her.

Memories of how devastated his father was in the tragic loss of his son haunted her. The strength of the talisman proved much more powerful than she had anticipated. Yet another thought corrupted this. The enchantment was meant to shield Pierce from sorrows and terrors.

"What do you remember from your childhood?" she curiously asked.

A grin burst from Pierce as he recalled his memories. "I remember spending the warm seasons on my grandfather's farm. We were constant companions, feeding the animals and laboring in the fields. The warmest days found us frolicking in the cool waters of a pond. Evenings were spent playing chess and stargazing. And there was always a bedtime story."

Brianna's suspicions found regretful confirmation. Pierce's lifetime memories, with exception of his grandfather, held such sorrow for him that the talisman withheld even the slightest recollections of his parents and the life he led with them. The mask he presented to her when they first met hid such unrivaled sadness. Her heart broke for him.

"What is your most recent memory?"

Softly he kissed her before responding, "The pleasure of your skin against mine."

Brianna rested her head down upon his chest, her hand roaming until feeling the beating of his heart. The clash of branches against the windowpanes lured her eyes to the window. A nagging feeling that they were being watched passed through her thoughts. Yet Pierce's gentle kiss upon her head lured her away from this notion.

Chapter Seven

Brianna reluctantly pulled free from Pierce's embrace, rising from her bed. After their bath, they had both fallen asleep within each other's arms under the comfort of the quilts. So soundly was his sleep he offered no reaction when she placed a kiss upon his lips. Silently she dressed and then heading for the door. With the wooden box in hand, she turned back to look at him before leaving the warmth of the cottage.

It was her intention to visit Shallow Hill under the guise of night, when the spirits were most active. The moon overhead was one day removed from being full. In the crispness of the chilled air, the shimmering stars rivaled the lunar glow. The exhale of her warm breath momentarily clouded her vision before rapidly vanishing. After taking a single step, her departure was halted when she noticed traces of footsteps in the snow near the window where there should not have been.

"Well... well; out for a stroll... in the moonlight, my dear." The sound of Ezekiel Fagan's voice chilled her more than any frigid wind ever could. "Ah; and... what have we here? Were you planning to return this to me… tonight?"

Brianna's hands trembled in their touch of his wooden box.

Stepping out from behind her, Ezekiel Fagan slowly moved to face her, the wickedness of his smile displaying nothing less than menace. His penetrating eyes seared through her, fueling the depths of her fear.

"Perhaps… there is something else… stolen from me… you desire to return. Possibly he rests… within this *charming* cottage of yours?" The marauders snuck behind her, forcefully grasping her arms and muffling her startled screams with their hands. Wrenching the wooden box from her, Egan returned it to Ezekiel Fagan. Suffering great pain from their force restraint of her body, her cries of agony could barely be heard.

"*Gentlemen*, we do not wish… to damage such a wild flower," he admonished the marauders. He ran his skeletal-like hand through her hair before tracing it down her cheek. "You do so… remind me of your mother. Such a tragedy it was… her untimely death… and that of your father as well. Such a tale of romance was theirs, vowing to find each other… in death… after both *unfortunately* fell from High Cliff."

Brianna's struggling ceased. Her heart broke for her parents, thinking of them plunging to their death off High Cliff, a wind-battered point with jagged rocks protruded through violent ocean swells at its base. Though possible one might survive plummeting clear of the rocks, the powerful undertow would then claim the person's life. With her eyes piercing through him, Brianna silently vowed to avenge her parent's deaths until drawn away from her rage by Ezekiel Fagan's next words with the wickedness of his smile transcending to a deeper evil.

"This… rather quaint cottage of yours reminds me of a youthful tale. My dear, do you remember a story of children… who attempted to follow a trail of breadcrumbs? Such an epiphany… I have had. *Possibly* not a trail of breadcrumbs, but rather a trail of precious gems will be what he follows to find you." Struck with overwhelming fear, Brianna felt her heart in her throat when she was forcibly dragged away by the marauders while Ezekiel Fagan remained.

Despite her head being covered with a cloth sack, Brianna continued struggling while being carried away by both marauders. She fought in vain, attempting to gain release from their restraint, yet failing. Neither spoke a word to her or even shared words among themselves. Her fear intensified with each passing moment. It was not a fear for herself that she agonized over. Her thoughts were only for Pierce's safety. Overpowered by the men, her heart sank as she surrendered all hopes in coming to his rescue once more. To Brianna, all seemed lost.

Sometime later, the metallic shriek of hinges alerted her to their destination. She knew this noise. So many times in the past, the gates of the Wyndham Graveyard had emitted such complaints. Brianna ceased all struggling while listening for more sounds. Resounding faint spirit voices, captured over the treading of footsteps crushing layers of crisp snowfall, whispered alarming words. Feeling both men laboring to carry her, she soon realized the marauders had taken her to the Shallow Hill.

Released from their grip, she slammed hard against an unseen wood surface. Before her hands could free her head from the confines of the cloth sack, something loud echoed above her. Any traces of light shone through the material soon vanished as her body was enveloped in darkness. Frantically reaching her hand out she immediately grasped her understanding of where she had been dropped. The terrifyingly unmistakable sounds of shovels and the piling of dirt foretold of her being buried alive. No response would be offered to either her screams or incessant pounding upon the lid of her wooden tomb.

†††

A loud jarring sound startled Pierce from the depths of his sleep. Groggily he sat up in bed and attempted to focus on his surroundings. Looking to his right, he found Brianna missing from his side. What he discovered no longer missing were his metal leg braces which were at the foot of the bed next to his clothes.

Easing his body from under the quilts he quickly dressed before attaching his metal leg braces. Cautiously he stood up, regaining his bearing with their use. Pierce thoroughly searched the cottage for Brianna, finding no traces of her. Walking over to door, he pulled it open and shivered from the chilled night air's greeting.

Intending to close the door, Pierce stopped when his eyes captured sight of a golden coin at rest upon the snow. Reaching down to pick it up, he noticed a red colored gem, also at rest upon the snow, though a short ways away. He retrieved both only to find more. A trail of gems, coins, and various pieces of jewelry led away from the cottage and into the forest.

After pulling on his overcoat, Pierce followed the trail. Brilliant light from the moon bathed the landscape, making the gems and coins sparkle upon the crisp white ground. With each one he gathered, he placed them in his pockets while continuing onward.

Arriving at a small glen surrounded by trees, he spied a stag and a doe quietly standing out in the open, oblivious to his presence. For several moments, he lingered there watching them. As one took a step, the other followed this move as if they were bound to each other. The night appeared so very still for them as if holding back any disturbance that would corrupt their sacred grace.

Walking away, Pierce returned to the trail of gems, jewelry, and coins leading him deeper into the forest. The walls of trees lining the path grew dense as the reaching moonlit branches overhead cast jagged shadows upon the snowy lane. The distant hoot from an owl startlingly captured his attention as well.

Climbing to the crest of a knoll, Pierce recognized the destination where he had been led to. With the final gem in his grasp, he looked out toward the lustrous landscape of Shallow Hill. "Why have these coins and gems led to here?" he mumbled to himself.

†††

"There, there, my dear," Amelia's soothing spirit voice attempted to comfort Brianna. "See now, the digging has stopped."

In regaining some control, Brianna, too, heard the marauders had ceased in burying her. Why? What would have pulled them away from their task? They had only been laboring for a few moments, definitely not enough time to fully cover the coffin. Thinking fast, Brianna whispered, "Amelia, I beg you. Tell me what you see outside."

A dreadfully long moment of silence passed before the deep voice of Captain Bainbridge whisper to her. "Amelia shields her eyes out of fear."

"For what reason? *Please*! I must know what you see."

Believing he had left her, Brianna was just to scream out once more when his words stifled her cry. "The moonlight is so very brilliant tonight, reminiscent of a shadowy afternoon. The marauders have left you here. They are down the hill, waiting. No, *not waiting*, but rather hiding. Ezekiel Fagan lingers near the mausoleum. The stone door is open... and there is the flicker of light from inside. He is not alone. There is another man with him, a strange man… dressed as a hunter. He has been here before. The hunter is handing a purse to Ezekiel Fagan. Gold coins are being counter, many gold coins."

"What is inside the mausoleum?" Brianna frantically questioned.

"Shackles, chains, knives… and a whip," Captain Bainbridge responded. "A hundred candles must be lit inside, just as it was the last time."

"*The last time!*" Brianna frantically repeated in question.

"The young man was named Byron," Captain Bainbridge responded.

Tears welled in her eyes as she remembered encountering Byron's spirit in the funeral home. With every ounce of strength remaining, Brianna desperately pounded and kicked at the wooden coffin. A chill passed through her body while struggling for breath in the thinning air. One final thrust of her fist against the coffin lid caused a slight crack in the wood. Narrower than the width of a finger, the crack allowed precious air and moonlight to seep in. Brianna leaned her head up to breathe in the cold air. Peering upward, she caught sight of a single brilliant star overhead. Closing her eyes, she begged an impossible wish to be granted to her.

Chapter Eight

Pierce caught site of the faint flicker of light in the mausoleum's window. Believing that it was Brianna who had led him here, he confusingly whispered to himself, "Why did she venture there?" Descending to the knoll's bottom, he walked over to the graveyard's gate. The high pitched squeal of the hinges made him wince as he pushed the gates aside. The force of a strong breeze captured the fallen snow upon the hill, briefly suspending a glistening veil of it before releasing the shimmering snowflakes to fall to the ground. Though understanding an eerie silence within graveyards was not uncommon, Pierce's sense of apprehension grew with each step.

An unsuspecting thrust against his back sent him sprawling face first upon the ground. The weight of two large men held firm to him as he struggled to free himself. A large hand pinned his cheek against the snow. A moment later, a pair of black boots stopped in front of him.

Harshly dragged to his feet, the larger of the two men held Pierce while the other man grasped his face, forcing him to look straight ahead. There in front Pierce was a tall older man with long white hair and a devilish smirk.

"I simply… deplore the hostility my employees must inflict upon you… once more. I implore you to understand… that the nature of your abduction… is a business arrangement."

From behind this man appeared another man dressed in fox-hunt styling of clothes with his face shielded by a white mask.

Through this ordeal Pierce had no fear, although confusion clouded his thoughts as the enchantment upon the talisman held true to its potency. Even in the face of danger, he remained calm.

With his overcoat and shirt ripped off him, his body uncontrollably quaked in the chill of the frigid winter air. An inquisitive smile cast across the tall man's face as he reached out to touch the pocket watch hanging from around Pierce's neck. "I sincerely believe… that time has run out."

Once the talisman was stolen from him, overwhelming fear caused Pierce's eyes to bulge. Instantly, he remembered being assaulted near the river by the two men, feeling a rush of severe pain coursing through his body. Other memories also returned. The torturous agony of the horse's hoofs pummeling his legs robbed him of his breath, so excruciating was the sensation. He even felt a sting from the palm of Brianna's hand when she slapped his face. Emotional pain next gained prominence as he recalled his lonely childhood, his parents too devoted to their own lives to lavish any attention on him. Private schools and physical abuse at the hands of cruel classmates also haunted him. Tears streamed from his eyes as the emotional tempest wreaked havoc upon his memories.

The hunter maintained his silence as he motioned toward Pierce's metal leg braces. The first man interjected, "I believe they should remain on... to allow him a sporting chance. Should this endeavor end... abruptly... I fear you will deeply regret your decision. I imagine you wish to extract... every ounce of... *exquisite* terror from the depths of his soul."

From behind his back the tall man revealed a riding crop which he handed to the hunter. "Taste... of the forbidden fruit," the tall man sneered. Swiftly the hunter stuck Pierce twice across his chest, leaving stinging welts across his flesh. Doubling over in pain, Pierce fell to his knees.

Unexpectedly, the men released their hold on Pierce, stepping back before leaving the graveyard and locking the gates behind them. The taller man slowly wandered away, heading in the direction of Shallow Hill. As for the hunter, he silently moved several paces ahead as he remained facing away from Pierce.

†††

"Captain Bainbridge! Captain Bainbridge!" Brianna bellowed.

"Be still, my lady," his spirit voice frantically whispered to her. "Ezekiel Fagan approaches." A silent moment passed before he continued. "The hunt for your young gentleman friend will commence when the hour strikes one."

"Pierce is here!" After a moment of uncontrolled weeping passed, the clarity of Brianna's thoughts rapidly returned. "Captain Bainbridge, you can converse with him, assist him to hide and find escape."

"Only those whom have conversed with the dead once before would hear my words," he replied.

"Pierce will hear you. Go to him. Reveal yourself. I beg you."

†††

"Run! Hide!" Pierce desperately searched for the person who spoke these words to him, yet saw no one. Once more the voice echoed its warning. Heeding this command,

Pierce scurried behind a tall headstone nearest to him.

"There is no safety here. You must trust me. Make your way to the mausoleum. It may be your only hope."

The hunter had disappeared from sight. Peering in all directions, Pierce found no traces of him.

"Move quickly; he is coming!"

Falling to his knees, he crawled through the snow until he reached another large headstone shaped like a cross. As he turned his head to the right, an arrow slightly grazed his cheek before ricocheting of a smaller headstone. Blood seeped from the wound before freezing upon his skin. Dropping to his stomach, Pierce scurried farther away until he heard more words.

"Remove your leg braces. Their sounds betray you."

After rapidly unfastening them, he cast them aside.

"Take them with you. They could be used as a weapon."

Once Pierce had moved on to hide behind an enormous, though low in height headstone, he rested for a moment. He shuddered through fear and chills, the stinging of the freezing snow against his bare back and chest nearly unbearable. He understood, though, his survival would force him to endure this pain.

Through great risk, Pierce crossed a wide open space to a cluster of headstones. Attempting to move behind the largest, words of warning halted him.

"*Stop!* There is something buried beneath the snow."

Using one of his metal leg braces, Pierce reached out with it. Quickly an animal trap was triggered when touching the snow near him. The metal leg brace snapped in two pieces by the strength of the trap's iron jaws.

Frenzied movements concealed by several headstones paralyzed Pierce. His eyes widened with terror. Two large black hounds appeared before him, presenting their sharp white teeth through menacing snarls. Another rapid approach also captured his attention. Deafening bellows from the voice helping Pierce startled the beasts as their paws nervously pranced, their snarls altering to whimpers. With the bellows resounding out once more, the hounds bolted away in panic.

Pierce shielded himself behind the largest headstone protruding through a snowbank in this section of the graveyard. Spying out, he saw the hunter standing still, though visibly enraged. Off toward the direction the hounds had escaped to, the hunter silently moved beyond Pierce's current hiding place. As he passed by, Pierce caught sight of a large dagger within the hunter's grasp.

An intense gale propelled squalls of snow across the graveyard, reducing visibilities to only inches away. Even the glow of the moon was shrouded from view, casting the grounds into darkness.

"Now is your chance! Hurry!" the voice called out to Pierce.

The shadow of the mausoleum proved only a short distance away. Crawling forward into the snowy torrent, the howling wind rendered him deaf to all sounds. Squall after squall pounded his exposed torso. Just as his strength was almost gone, he touched the bottom step leading up to the mausoleum doors.

Fully exhausted, Pierce rolled over onto his back, glancing up toward the now visible moon. The gale had subsided enough to allow the moonlight to shine upon the taller headstones. A shimmering from above him caught his attention. Two massive icicles dangled precariously above the steps, the gusting wind shifting them as if they were chimes. Recognizing the danger, Pierce pulled himself up the steps, coming to rest against the freezing stone facade. With difficulty, he reattached his remaining leg brace and stood up. His gaze was instantly drawn to a flash of light. Somewhat suspended in time as its trajectory appeared slow, the metal from the thrown dagger reflected the moonlight, slicing through the squall. A searing pain forced him to his knees as the dagger's sharp blade impaled his thigh. Robbed of his breath and strength, Pierce cast a weary glance out toward the fading veil. There in front of him was the hunter's silhouette. Deliberately slow steps were taken by the hunter until he found his way to the bottom steps.

Depleting his last ounce of strength, Pierce struggled to stand before the hunter, summoning as much courage and defiance as he was able. Leaning with his back pressed against the wall, he awaited his fate. The hunter's steps halted with the deluge of more gust-driven snow. A moonlit sparkle upon the larger of the two icicles captured Pierce's glance. Wrenched from its hold of the mausoleum roof, the icicled rapidly speared down, stabbing the hunter in his chest. Falling to the ground, his body convulsed for only a few moments. Pierce slumped down with his back against the wall. The blood from the wound had instantly frozen on his skin. Gritting his teeth, he grasped the dagger's hilt, pulling with all his might until free of it.

Chapter Nine

Appearing oblivious to the hunt, Ezekiel Fagan stood upon Shallow Hill, gazing out toward the moon's reflection upon the frozen Warwick River. No words were spoken by him. He simply stood there waiting. Were it a sign of some sort he was expecting, the sign he received certainly may not have been what he might have anticipated. The impact of the shovel's blade forced him to his knees before he unconsciously slumped forward.

"Over here! Make haste!" a voice called out.

Staggering over to the fresh grave, Pierce dropped to his knees and began digging snow and dirt away with his bare hands. An exhausted smile of relief cast across his face as he heard Brianna's pounding and cries of help. The ill-constructed coffin burst open from the force of her final thrust against the lid. Tossing the wooden remnants from the lid aside, Pierce pulled Brianna up but then collapsed into her embrace.

He blinked; his smile fading. Desperately Brianna whispered, "Stay with me," as he became unresponsive. Knowing both her cottage and the city were too far away to take him, Brianna frantically searched for refuge. Exhaling her relief at spotting the faint flicker of light nearby, down the hill she lugged his body until they had reached the mausoleum. Dragging him inside, she found a place in the farthest corner for him to rest. The numerous lit candles, as well as flames from a stone fireplace provided comfortable heat. Removing her cloak, Brianna draped it over Pierce. Though now unconscious with his breathing shallow, she knew he was still alive. Bloody stains on his trousers alerted her to his leg injury. Tearing at the hem of her dress, Brianna made a tourniquet for his wound. Softly she placed a kiss upon his forehead before standing up.

Halting in her steps, Brianna's jaw dropped in horror by what she failed to see when they had entered. She was amidst a torture chamber. Captain Bainbridge had revealed what was here inside the mausoleum. Yet hearing and seeing were vastly different. Her chin quivered as she held back her tears. Brianna could not bear to touch the chains and shackles that were meant for Pierce. Had they been used for Byron? She attempted to force this terrifying though from her mind, yet it lingered.

Sorrow rapidly turned to rage. Retribution for these horrific acts fueled her resolve. Certain that Peirce would not soon awaken, Brianna again kissed his forehead before stepping outside the mausoleum. There upon then moonlit ground was the hunter's corpse. Before reaching here, Brianna noticed a shallow grave that had been dug next to the one she had been placed in. With no more than a quick moment's thought, Brianna determined the shallow grave would become the hunter's final resting place. Only a short amount of time passed before she thrust his body into it. No final rites were offered to his revolting soul as she believed he failed to deserve such absolution. No efforts were made to bury the hunter's body, allowing full exposure to the night's bitter chill.

Subtle movements of Ezekiel Fagan's head were met once more with the blade of the shovel against his skull. Certain he had returned to unconsciousness, Brianna extracted her next act of retribution. Though much taller than the wooden coffin could hold, she somehow manipulated his arms and legs in such a way as to fit him inside. His agitated mumbling alerted her that he would soon awaken. Lowering the remnants of the coffin lid over him, she covered all but one small space with dirt and snow. Brianna stepped back and waited.

Meandering away, she kicked something partially covered by the snow. She soon held Pierce's stolen pocket watch. Her understanding of what this meant brought tears to her eyes. All she had hoped to shield from him had been revealed when it was taken from him. In a mere matter of minutes he must have endured a lifetime's remembrance of both physical and emotional anguish.

While standing there, Brianna gazed upon a world forever changed for her. It was not as if everything appeared new, but rather how she now saw truth and fallacy. Ezekiel Fagan, a man feared by all, was brought down by simply striking his skull with a shovel. The hunter, a rather unassuming man she had seen many times strolling through the city, proved to be one she never would have suspected of such depraved and violent acts. And then there was Pierce. How was it possible to fall so deeply in love with someone she had known for only a short time?

Brianna's gaze fell further upon her surroundings. The silhouettes of several snow geese passed by the moon as they disappeared into the night. The moonlit sheen upon the frozen Warwick River offered the appearance of delicate glass. The faint glow of streetlamps from the city's edge corrupted the darkness of the night sky. Visible exhales of her warm breath clouded her vision before vanishing.

Her waiting abruptly came to a halt upon hearing a thump from Ezekiel Fagan's coffin. More forceful sounds emanated as she suspected he had regained consciousness. Peering down toward the dirt, Brianna captured the sight of Ezekiel Fagan's eye gazing upon her from the crack in the lid. It expressed nothing less than uncharacteristic vulnerable fear.

Her body quaked with a frightened chill when Ezekiel Fagan bellowed out laughter. Through the casket lid, Brianna heard him utter with his usual menacing tone, "I… would not be so hasty… to silence the one… who could reveal what truly happened to your parents. I could keep their final moments here… in my soon-to-be-grave."

"*Speak—demon*," Brianna demanded.

"Only by releasing me… will I tell you… that which your heart desires."

From one of the pockets on her dress, Brianna pulled out a polished black pendant in the shape of a scarab. Running her fingertips over the smooth surface, she remember where it had been pinned on the white turban her father wore when performing his magical illusions. Oh, how he treasured it, a gift from the caliph of a desert kingdom where he had once performed. Her father always kept it close. Having discovered both it and her mother's locket in the box of jewelry Ezekiel Fagan had robbed from the graves, she knew they were both dead before he had revealed the how and where of it. Summoning the resolve not to give in to the temptation of hearing more of Ezekiel Fagan's lies, Brianna dismissed his ploy for release. Yet he persisted.

"Have you found… your mother's crystal pendant?"

Recalling memories of this piece of jewelry, crafted from clear polished prisms, Brianna fondly remembered how when the prisms captured light, her mother's silk clothing would appear immersed in a kaleidoscope of vibrant colors. Although longing to have this remembrance from her mother, Brianna dismissed the notion to ask of its whereabouts, thinking it only another trick by him in gaining release from the coffin.

Distracted within her thoughts of once more mourning the loss of her father and mother, Ezekiel Fagan's continued ramblings were incomprehensible to Brianna. The pounding of his fist against the casket's lid soon, however, returned her attention to him. Continuing to reject all notions of releasing him, Brianna confronted him one final time.

"Welcome to Shallow Hill, Ezekiel Fagan. You should take care to rest before your journey to hell."

After speaking this last word, Brianna shoveled the final heap of dirt upon the casket. The crack sealed, as did Ezekiel Fagan's fate. She wandered away before his frantic pounding and muffled bellows ceased.

The slurred drunken sounds of singing alerted Brianna to her final retribution. With stealth, she moved soundlessly until she found a hiding place behind the largest headstone nearest to the graveyard gates. Hysterical laughing from the marauders echoed out as Egan attempted to open the locked gate. After trying several keys, the last one opened the lock with ease. The high-pitched shriek of the hinges caused everyone to wince.

Honorably bowing, although nearly falling over, Peter politely said, "After you, most esteemed Mister Craven."

"No, no, after you, most drunken Mister Borgan. I insist," Egan responded with his own bow.

Their uncontrolled hysterics returned as they draped arms around each other, staggering along the road.

"Fools," Brianna mumbled in disgust.

Quietly she made her move as they passed by. Having become quite skilled in the improper use of a shovel, Brianna was able to knock both marauders out with a single swing, their bodies instantly thumping down to the ground. As she moved cautiously around them, she spied a wheelbarrow they had left just outside the gates. She also discovered Pierce's snow covered shirt and overcoat, its pockets still bursting with coins and gems.

After making two grueling trips to the mausoleum, her last retribution found perversion with its execution. Once sober, the marauders would discover their naked bodies bound by shackles and chains. Being that the next day was a remembrance day, when the priest led a pilgrimage to the graveyard, Brianna was most certain their lustful discovery would yield severe consequences. Before leaving them, she bowed to the drunken fools.

"Sleep well my fine gentlemen. For when the day breaks, you will feel the sting of revenge, one not even your vile master can save you from."

Chapter Ten

Singing a lullaby reminiscent of a folkloric-hymn, the lilt of Brianna's voice captured the sweet and melancholy nuances of the lyrics as she tenderly stroked Pierce's hair. The essence of chamomile filled the air, both of them soothed by the aroma.

The movement of his head was followed by the sight of his beautiful eyes. The sleepy smile he cast to her was met by the touch of her lips to his. Easing down under the quilts, she allowed her naked body to be lured into his warm embrace. Her fingers came to rest upon his bare chest as she searched for the beating of his heart.

Brianna felt Pierce's hand caress her. She was enraptured by his pleasant touch. She gazed into Pierce's eyes, beguiled by their gentleness and serenity. She desperately wanted nothing more than to continue watching them, yet a thought burning her tongue found its voice. Hesitantly Brianna broke their silence.

"So… what comes now? I met your father at the graveyard. He appeared sincerely distraught over your death. He should know you are alive."

Exhaling, Pierce responded, "So I may return to a lifeless existence?" He softly caressed her freckled cheek before pushing her red mane from her face. "Other than the times with my grandfather, the only life I have ever known, ever truly felt, is with you. Without you… I would be no more than one of the spirits who lingers upon Shallow Hill."

Leaning over, Pierce shared a passionate kiss with Brianna.

Reminded of his grandfather, Brianna reached over to the table next to her bed and returned Pierce's pocket watch to him. For a moment, he held it in the palm of his hand, studying it.

"You were correct. Every terrible and sad memory returned in a matter of minutes when this was stolen from me. I remembered the loneliness I felt as a child. Wandering from room to room at the estate, I would search for my parents only to discover so many closed doors. They were devoted to both profession and society. Paraded before important people when my mother threw extravagant parties, I was a mere trophy for display before being cast aside once they had convinced others in their roles as adoring parents. I felt as I was no more than an afterthought for them.

"The memory from being injured by the horse was brutal to endure once more. The pain never seemed the worst of it. It was the shame of seeing the disappointment upon my parent's faces when I first wore my leg braces, unbearable to watch. No more would I be paraded before the social elite. I remained hidden in my room for the duration of such events.

"By the age of twelve, my parents sent me away to a boarding school. Seldom ever did I return home, not even for holidays. I was ridiculed and tortured by some of my classmates. My attempts to defend myself... never found success. I sought the aid of the chancellor and faculty. Once I even once spoke to my parents about this and suffered admonishment by all for not attempting to fit in."

Brianna soothingly touched his cheek.

"The worst memory of —all—was not when taken by those men. Hardly any of that holds memories for me,' he said.

"What was your worst memory?" Brianna quietly asked.

"When I left you at the graveyard after we first met. I never thought I would see you again."

Brianna melted deeper into his loving embrace, kissing his shoulder.

"My existence as the son of Malcolm and Beatrice Fleming ended many years ago. Please do not think of me as cruel that I take his sorrow lightly. I mourned my own passing as their son so long ago. From that moment on… I have existed within my own Shallow Hill."

He leaned over to place another passionate kiss to her lips.

"May I stay here with you—as your husband—if you would have me?" Pierce asked. "I cannot promise you a life of opulence and privilege—as I have nothing other than my heart to offer you."

Brianna thought of the gems and coins she found in his pockets, a fortune to live off for years to come. She smiled. In truth, she only desired his heart.

Withholding her response to his marriage proposal, Brianna said, "I wish for you to come with me." Prying herself from his embrace, she rose from her bed and began dressing. Seeing his confusion, she begged, "*please.*"

"Very well," Pierce grinningly responded.

He sat up, reaching for his clothes and his one remaining leg brace. Once dressed, Brianna offered him a crutch her father once used after suffering an ankle injury. Standing and walking somewhat unsteady, Brianna held on to him, leading Pierce outside and on down a lane shaded from the midday sunlight. Hearing the chirping of birds and scampering of small animals hidden in dense brush, they silently walked on until a gusting wind disturbed the overhead forest canopy.

Less than an hour later after emerging from the forest's edge, with difficulty Brianna and Pierce climbed a hill to stand before a single pale-white barked tree barren of summer leaves. Assaulted by tempestuous winds while nearly deafened by the roar of wave colliding against jagged rocks, Pierce called out, "What is this place?"

"This is High Cliff," Brianna answered. "This is where my parents are."

Pierce tightened his grip on her hand and smiled reassuringly.

"Before I accept your proposal of marriage, I wish to seek their blessings... should their spirits linger here," she said.

"Why would their spirits linger here? Is this where they are buried?"

Brushing wind-blown strands of hair away from her face, Brianna answered, "No, their bodies were never allotted the sanctity of burial. They were pushed off the edge of the cliff, as revealed by Ezekiel Fagan."

"And you believe him, a man whose words are corrupted by lies?"

Reaching into the pocket of her dress, Brianna withdrew her mother's locket and her father's scarab pendant. Holding them out to Pierce, she responded, "These belonged to my parents. I found them among the treasures Ezekiel Fagan had stolen from the dead."

Caressing her cheek, Pierce silently attempted to comfort her.

Pulling away from him, she stepped closer to the edge of the cliff and closed her eyes. Believing that by their horrific passings, her mother and father's spirits would be bound to this place, Brianna attempted to block out the roaring wind in trying to hear her parent's voices. Yet following a few minutes of deep concentration, neither uttered a single word to her. In truth, a sense of relief flooded over her in understanding that her parents were not suffering the same lonely fate as those bound to Shallow Hill. They had been called home to Heaven. That she was certain of.

When she opened her eyes, she watched Pierce hobble closer to her. "I could not hear their voices." Brianna stopped a tear from falling down her cheek. "Neither is here."

Pointing to her chest, Pierce commented, "Yes they are. They both exist in your heart. Ask your question. I believe you will know their response."

Before speaking her request for their approval of her marrying Pierce, when glancing over his shoulder, Brianna's eyes grew large with fear, seeing the ghostly apparition of Ezekiel Fagan charging toward them. Never before had she witnessed such an expression of insanity. To her, it seemed that time had slowed and she was doomed to being captured within the wickedness he so clearly shone.

After seeing Ezekiel Fagan's spirit pass through Pierce, Brianna stumbled back in shock. Losing her footing, she fell of the edge of the cliff, the roaring wind deafening her as she plummeted. Reaching her hand out, surprisingly she grasped a branch protruding the cliff wall, which stopped her from falling to the jagged rocks and ocean swell below.

She frantically looked about, but Ezekiel Fagan's malicious spirit had disappeared. Yet, for a moment, she panicked when a hand reached out over the cliff's edge.

"Grab my hand!" Pierce yelled down to her.

Battered by the strength of the gales assaulting the cliff, Brianna could barely reach her free hand up. And when finally able to do so, she found her reach just short of his fingers.

Fighting for breath and feeling around, attempting to gain some footing on the stone, Brianna's struggles halted when she was blinded by a burst of light. Looking to her right, she caught sight of a kaleidoscope of colors shining through the prisms of her mother's crystal pendant, tightly entwined between small thin branches. Yet as she looked closer, her heart sank in recognizing that it was not branches holding her mother's pendant, but the skeletal remnants of a human hand. Turning forward, what breath she held rushed from her lungs in seeing that the branch she clung to was in truth the bones of the arm attached to the skeletal hand. Knowing how much her mother cherished the crystal prism pendant, deep in her heart Brianna believed her mother's arm had halted her fall.

Her sight was one more lured upward. She saw Pierce lowering his metal leg brace to cover the distance separating his hand from hers. Grasping at it with her free hand, she found success in prying the pendant from her mother's brittle fingers and holding tightly to it. Letting go of the bones of her mother's arm, she grabbed the leg brace. Noticing the strain on Pierce's face in pulling her up, she feared he might lose the strength to continue. Yet when looking into his eyes, she saw not desperation, but resolve and love.

He will not fail me.

Within an inch of reaching the top of the cliff, Brianna discovered a golden medallion, with the profane image of an evil fiery dragon etched into its tarnished surface. Instantly she knew this to be the treasure binding Ezekiel Fagan's spirit to High Cliff. Somehow either her mother or father must have stolen it from him and tossed it over the edge. Letting go for only a moment from Pierce's leg brace, Brianna took hold of the medallion. Then casting it out in the air, she watched it fall until disappearing amidst the impacting waves below, forever exiling his spirit to the ocean depths.

With a large full moon hanging high in the night sky, a lustrous lunar glow bathed the hallowed grounds of Shallow Hill, offering a late afternoon impression to the frosted white stone garden. Stray snowflakes descended from above, as if they were a delicate dust falling from the stars. Brianna held her silence while wandering from one grave marker to the next, reading the names and dates etched upon their surfaces, engraving each into her memory. Though she could hear the spirit voices calling out to her, she did not speak to them, having not found the courage to say goodbye.

Hearing the metallic clinking of Pierce's new leg braces, she exhaled when he comfortingly wrapped his arms around her from behind.

"I thought I might find you here," he whispered in her ear. Gently running one hand over her stomach, he asked, "Do you believe our child will someday discover the gift to converse with the departed?"

"We all have this ability," Brianna replied while covering his hand with hers. "It is not an exclusive gift. We simply need only to express what our heart's wish to say what is necessary. The spirits will listen. Yet only those with deep warm hearts will hear that which is spoken back, though not so much in words, but rather subtle responses such as intuition coming to us or the faint caresses of the wind against our skin. For others, some may never experience these sweet responses for their minds and souls are burdened by unyielding logic and disbelief, rendering their hearts cold and shallow."

Jeffery Martin Botzenhart

I hope you like *Shallow Hill*, my first attempt at writing a scary story. As an author, I've written stories in the genres of steampunk, historical and contemporary romance, and young adult science fiction. I just write what comes to my head. Away from writing I'm an artist, husband, father, soccer coach and holder of a Bachelor's degree in International Relations. Enough about me, I want to know about you. What's it like being you? What secrets do you want to share? I don't judge. Come on, just tell me. It's not like I'm going to tell anyone. You're talking to a page in a book. If it answers you—you probably should be worried.

Social Media Links

Twitter: https://twitter.com/JBotzenhart @JBotzenhart

Facebook:
https://www.facebook.com/jefferymartinbotzenhartwritingjourney/

If you enjoyed this story, check out these other Solstice Publishing books by Jeffery Martin Botzenhart:

Painted Desert

Sung with haunting vocals, a spares fragile melody strummed in the dark on a guitar can be one of many disguises for the lonely. Others, either victim of circumstance or of their own devices stay hidden behind colorful masks and pretty decorations to shield their pain. Yet these masquerades hold flaws for hearts searching to heal, revealing not desolate barren souls as any more than a painted desert, but desert angels waiting to lead the lost to the light.

https://bookgoodies.com/a/B072MZY1FK

Daybreak (Nightfall Book 1)

Amidst a world of cyber surveillance and advancing technology of 2035 San Francisco, Sebastian, a teen runaway, innocently access a sophisticated virtual reality program. The breach of this data proves the catalyst in unraveling corporate and government sanctioned deception of the most unimaginable type. And along with his computer hacker friend, Scotty, both are thrust into a dangerous conspiracy, linking them to a source exposing the truth.

https://bookgoodies.com/a/B073SB9BXG

Creature of the Night

Some souls were not meant to lead lives in the sun. They remain hidden within dark realms in fear of being seen and misunderstood. That is Ian's fate after suffering at the hands of a demon blinded by rage and sorrow. Yet there exists a threat in the light, spreading lies driven by fear in warning others to be weary of the unknown prowling the depths of the forest. The unyielding belief in the justification of cruelty in seeking to end that which has been branded as profane proves all consuming. When entering the forest after twilight to pronounce final judgement for those in hiding, the threshold of good versus evil is blurred by the righteous. And thus a question may be asked. Who is the true creature of the night?

https://bookgoodies.com/a/B075ZZMGGN

Harvest Fever

Bullied by classmates and abused by his stepdad, seventeen year old Orrville Fletcher plans to leave his run-down home outside Birchwood Hollow, Tennessee once he turns eighteen. But one night after fighting off his stepdad, his escape from this small remote town in Appalachia is halted by an unimaginable invasion of space aliens, leading him to revelations of an unexpected truth.

https://bookgoodies.com/a/B074JZV44F

www.ingramcontent.com/pod-product-compliance
Lightning Source LLC
Chambersburg PA
CBHW070042030726
47506CB00003B/833

* 9 7 8 1 6 2 5 2 6 7 2 2 1 *